NARNOLS BLUMBLUMS & FRIENDS

by Dr. Vicky Ciocon-Heler, Ed. D

A few poems to make you smile, to be the happy person I know you to be – dearest Witty – May 2019

love – Vicky

NARNOLS, BLUMBLUMS AND FRIENDS
Copyright © 2019 by Dr. Vicky Ciocon-Heler Ed.D.

Library of Congress Control Number: 2018955895

ISBN-13:
Paperback: 978-1-64398-292-2
PDF: 978-1-64398-293-9
ePub: 978-1-64398-294-6
Kindle: 978-1-64398-295-3

Printed in the United States of America

LitFire
PUBLISHING

LitFire LLC
1-800-511-9787
www.litfirepublishing.com
order@litfirepublishing.com

Contents

To my Jatou,
my Jacou,
my Michou,
my Teebou
—all my love

Dr. Vicky Ciocon-Heler Ed.D. was born and raised in Manila, Philippines. She completed her undergraduate studies from Maryknoll College in Child Study. She continued graduate studies in Northern California at Stanford University and two more Jesuit institutions. She has more than forty-six years of work experience with preschoolers. She has owned her own Infant-Toddler Center, Lilliput, for more than thirty-five years. Another children's book Paquita-Gamita's Wiggling is available in Amazon too. She lives in Palo Alto, California with her family.

SATURDAY'S PRESS

When Saturday comes, I will be a mess.
I have to wear my Sunday's best.
My mom will put me to a test.
And hopes I stop being a pest.

Took the birds out of their nest!
Cut sis' hair on her behest!
Spat the spinach I detest!
Shouted and screamed out of duress!

Now Saturday's here and I'm a mess.
We have to visit my aunt Celeste.
Who's prim and proper like a duchess.
And she just wants to rest, rest, rest.

I tried to sit still at mom's behest.
I truly tried my very best!
I didn't want to be a pest.
I pretended to be quiet in a nest.

Spilled tea on my Sunday's best!
Then gulped the crumpets and all the rest!
Laughed loud,
Guffawed,
All in jest!
The rest I leave for you to guess!

No more Saturday's press.
No need to wear my Sunday's best.
No more invitations from Aunt Celeste.
I failed mom's test –
I can attest!

TEMPER! TEMPER!

What is all this gibberish?
this babbling?
this gurgling?

What is all the fuss?
the whining?
the growling?

What is all the nonsense?
the shouting!
the yelling!

What is all the temper!
the glaring!
the crying!

You'll get tired.
You'll get blue.
You'll get moody – boo, hoo, hoo!

Just be calm.
Just be loose.
Just be happy – like a goose!

You'll forget to gibber, babble, gurgle.
You'll forget to whine and growl and
shout!
You'll forget to yell and glare and cry!
You'll forget 'cuz YOU DO CARE.

Then you'll wonder what the fuss,
the nonsense,
the temper was about!

Then you'll feel
so much, much better,
after all these silly banter!

COLORS

Orange and violet
Red and blue
Green and yellow
These are for you.

Purple and rose
Brown and gold
Silver and chartreuse
Lime and grey mold

Mauve and indigo
Magenta and teal
Black and white
Pink and oatmeal

Lemon sun
Metallic gun
Colors are fun.
They're for everyone.

Look around you
there's sky blue
marine blue too
cinnamon goo

Colors make the world happy.
Life is all beauty.
Colors are pretty.
They're there for you and me.

WAN DEM OL!

Lubock stuffs blumblums into his mouth.
Makren sucks narnols.
Glulic munches on mingis.
Blakor drinks maforinis.

Uhm,
Yum, yum,
Want some –
For my tum-tum!

Slurp,
Blurp,
Blimi, blami
Diggity - gum!

Zowie-wowie,
Raboom-boom,
Mingis crunchy,
Mouth happy.

No sippy-sips,
Big gulps only,
Glunk, glob, gling,
Ten maforinis for zing!

Blumblums,
Yum, yums,
Wowie treat,
For big teeth.

Wan som blumblums - say!
Wan som narnols, mingis, maforinis!
Borkel wan dem ol - TODAY!

BUSY BUNNIES

Five bunny friends were busy –
Playing video games,
Munching chips and cookies,
Drinking juice and soda,
While they sat, sat, sat.

Five bunny friends were busy –
Playing board games,
Munching chocolate and candy,
Drinking juice and soda,
While they sat, sat, sat.

Five bunny friends were busy –
Watching T.V.,
Munching doughnuts and fries,
Drinking milk, juice and soda,
While they sat, sat, sat.

Five bunny friends were busy –
Playing with computer games,
Chatting/texting on their cell phones,
E-mailing their other friends.
While they sat, sat, sat.

Five bunny friends were busy –
Surfing the web,
Yapping on the phone,
Hanging out with buddies,
While they sat, sat, sat.

Five bunny friends were tired –
And they went to bed –
To sleep, sleep, sleep.
zzzzzzz

TOO MUCH CLOTHING

Is it a thick mist?
Is it a heavy fog?
Or is this what they call the smog?

It certainly looks cold out there.
I can hardly see the roads.
There are fewer people walking too.
And the cars have hit the roads.

Pants and shirt,
Warm pullover,
Handy gloves,
Rubber boots,
Thermal socks,
And dressing time's over – Whew!

Put on your parka.
Wear your wool cap.
Cover your ears.
And your neck must be wrapped –
Oh, rat!

Is it a thick mist?
Is it a heavy fog?
Or is this what they call the smog?

There is too much bulk.
I look like the Hulk.
I can't balk. I can't walk.

Too much clothing is no fun.
Comfort's gone. There's none.
No ease when done.
Well... I'm gone.

NO THANK YOU

Teacher says –
Gracias to Malia
Merci to Camille
Arigato to Yume
Danke to Lukas
Salamat to Chachi
Thank you to everybody
Toda to me

Thank you/Toda to me
Thank you/Gracias to Malia
Danke, Arigato, Merci
Thank you, Salamat, Toda to me.

All day I hear thank you, thank you –
for good reading
for good singing
for good dancing
for good eating
for good playing
for good sleeping

I think I know what it means now;
when to use it,
It's a good thing.
But — I don't want to say
thank you!
And – I don't want to say
Toda!

I'm two! Only two.
I say Tetuu! Only when I want to!

TETUU!

CHRISTMAS CHEER

Christmas is coming near;
There's lots of holiday cheer.
The children are busy - getting ready -
so have no fear

Their faces smiling
Their eyes all aglow
They chatter and prattle
Getting ready for the morrow

Papier-maches, wreaths
Crepe ribbons around
Red and green colored balls
Decorations abound

The children are busy,
are giddy, are silly.
Their hands glue, cut, color.
Help mom with decor.
They cook and bake.
Lots of cookies and cake.

They checked the presents
in different sizes.
All wrapped - all surprises!
Mesmerizes! Tantalizes!

They laugh and they giggle.
Dance round the Christmas tree.
Their joy is contagious.
They laugh loud with glee!

SPORTS AND BALLS

Balls in sports
All kinds of balls

Shoot the three-pointer.
Kick the winning goal.
Hit down the line.
Go for the touchdown.

Hit a homerun.
Swim to the goal.
Aim for the corners.
Spike the ball.

Did you guess the sports?
Can you name the balls?
Basketball
Soccer
Tennis
Football
Baseball
Water Polo
Ping Pong
Volleyball

What would these sports be without the balls.
All kinds -
All makes -
All Sizes -
Of Balls

BABY TALK

"AHDONNOMMTATA?"
"DATDATDAT - DISDISDIS"
"UHMSEECACAOWIE"
"PISBOOKMEMEREEDBOOK"

Well - I listen, listen, listen.
I talk; I ask; I repeat.
I nod; I smile to encourage her to stop
"talking" with a beat!

I try and try to talk to her.
She shouts, repeats her words.
But I just tell her sorry,

nothing, nothing
nothing works.

And - then one day it happened -

Heads Click
Eyes Bright
Words Clear

Big Smiles
Eyes Twinkling
Mouth Moving
Hands Pointing

WE WERE TALKING TO EACH OTHER!

"andonnommtata?"
I don't know where mama is?
"datdatdat; disdisdis"
that, that, that; this, this, this
"uhmseecacaowie"
Uh, look at Becca; she gave me an owie.
"pisbookmemereedbook"
Please read me a book; read that book!
Now - wasn't that easy!?

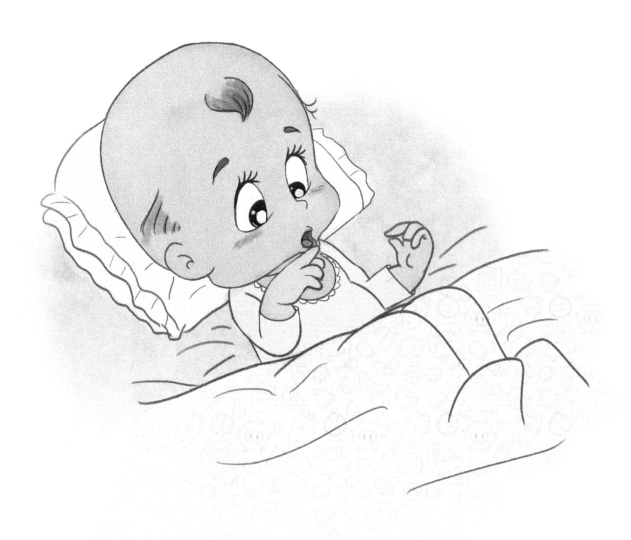

THE MOVIES

Watch the movies
View the make-believe
Enjoy the fantasy
Let your imagination fly

The scarred boy riding on a strange bird?
The captain looking for pirates
to man a ship?
Have you seen the talking animals with
their favorite medic?
Were you amazed at the gorgeous webs
with the special words?
How would you like to be one of seven
with a singing nanny?
Would you like to climb a treehouse on
an Isolated island?
Did you sigh when they shared a
spaghetti noodle?

Action, Characters, Music, Stories
Strange places, Secret sites,
Fantastical delights!

Comedies, Tragedies, Adventure to boot
You'll find these in the movies –
No doubt about this and more's afoot!
So, look around you
At the movie about you
Your home, your life
Your family, friends too!
It's all about you.
You're the hero –
It's true!
So enjoy your movie –
The movie made by you!

SEE YOU LATER, ALLIGATOR

Press the button with the arrow that goes down
You're in a hurry and you want to go downtown

What's the matter, elevator, you're so late in coming
I can hear you though - humming, shining,
softly sighing,
seemingly pining?
sounds like you're aching...

What a life you must be leading
always waiting, waiting, waiting
going up and going down
watching people entering, leaving
wondering why they never speak
All they do is stare and nary a squeak!

Press the button with the arrow that goes down
I'm impatient; I can't wait; I want to go to town

Wheeeeee - schhhhuck ....why you're just in time
you never fail to come

up and down
wheeeeee - schhhhuck
down and up
wheeeeee - schhhhuck

that's the faithful elevator
see you later, alligator

SIX BY SIX

Snickerdoodles, cheerios,
Pine nuts, pomegranates,
Apples, and some tartlets,
Crackers, peanut butter,
Mangoes and papayas,
Smores, and dates; that's a lot!

Roses, daisies, tulips,
Petunias, marigolds,
Asters, pansies, lilies,
Lantanas, and poppies,
Orchids, daffodils too,
Flowers and that's enough!

It's easy to remember -
how to make a list grow long.
It's not as hard as writing lyrics and
notes on scales
for a song!

Choose a theme
Pull some papers from a ream
Think up a catchy scheme
Smile, smile, and beam

The lists may sound quite silly -
Writing a poem willy-nilly –

But it's really just an exercise -
With six per line -
With only six lines -
to be precise!

MY FRIENDS

My friends like me.
They tell me so.
They tell me I'm me.
So they like me - you see.

Clumsy
Silly
Happy
Snotty

Busy
Bratty
Geeky
Smelly

Noisy
Grabby
Kissy
Bendy

I'm all these.
I'm also a tease.
But I'm loyal,
I'm kind and gentle.
And I'm quick to make up with a kiss.

That's me; all me;
I'm telling you so.
My friends like me,
because I'm just me!

OWIES

Owies, Ouchies, Booboos, Bumps!
Scratches, Gashes, Great big Lumps!

Open Wounds, Bites, Hard Squeezes too;
Shouts, Screams, Faces all blue!

Owies no fun
from friends and foe!
Scratches, Bites,
from cats, thorns – Oh Woe!

Pushing, Bopping, Poking – Oh Dear!
Pulling Hair, Grabbing, Nasty Sneer!

Small Falls, Stumbles, Hitting the Walls,
Accidents, Losing Balance, Falling down,
Getting hit by Balls!
Terrible!
Horrible!
Nightmares all!
I'm leaving town!

Owies, Ouchies, Booboos, A Large Bump!
Scratches, Gashes, A Great Big Lump.

No one likes them –
They make me cry.
I hurt; I ouch;
They make me fry.

Throw them in the dump!

KERLONGS

Six Capoops from the land of Grimobir,
work hard in the forest.
They chat all day long;
No time for a song;
They chat to sort Kerlongs.

Chat, Chat, Chat, Chat –
Sort, Sort, Sort.
Chat, Chat, Chat, Chat –
Sort, Sort, Sort.

Kerlongs, Kerlongs, Kerlongs –
All day long
Kerlongs, Kerlongs, Kerlongs –
no time for a song.

Kerlongs are chatterwords for Capoops.
Capoops make them in their heads.
Then, they fall on the ground.
They drop from their mouths.
Chat, Chat, Chat, Chat –
Sort, Sort, Sort.
Kerlongs all day long –
no time for a song.

Six hard-working Capoops from Grimobir.
Watch as the Kerlongs drop.
Six hard-working Capoops from Grimobir
Watch as the last Kerlong drops.

What are they staring at?
Why are they still?
The chatting has stopped –
The sorting is done.
All Kerlongs have dropped –
What are they staring at?
Why are they still?

Oh, look at the Kerlongs –
on the ground left to right –
from top to bottom,
on grids real tight.
Kerlongs on the grids are hidden there.
Capoops have to find them, not look
elsewhere.

Capoops need to chat, to sort, to go on.
Capoops need Kerlongs to continue on.

Find them from the grid
to know what they are.
Find Kerlongs for the Capoops
so they can start over.

P	S	S	D	I	S	M
L	O	C	C	M	R	O
F	A	M	R	R	E	R
P	C	T	B	E	M	S
L	G	O	M	T	W	Q
N	R	A	S	O	T	S

Answer: SCREWS

NAPTIME

Ho hum.. .Ho hum...
I'm sleepy, I think
I'll take a nap...

Ho hum.. .Ho hum...
I'm sleepy, I think
I'll go to sleep!

Ho hum ... Ho hum...
I'm sleepy
But I can't sleep!

Ho hum ... ho hum...
I'm sleepy, I think
I'll suck my thumb...

Ho hum.. .ho hum.
I'm tweaking my hair.
I don't have a care.
I'm trying to sleep.
Mr. Sandman sprinkle dust on me!

Where's my blankie?
Where's my bunnie?
Where's my monkie?
Where's my dollie?

Ho hum ... Ho hum...
I need my nap.
I'm such a sap.
I have to nap. Ho hum...

HOP/SKIP

Hop, hop, hop
Front and back
Hop, hop, hop
Side to side

Hop, hop, hop
Here and there
Hop, hop, hop
Like a top

Hop, hop, hop
With both your feet
Hop, hop, hop
Two feet to the beat

Take your time
Take your time
Skip, skip, skip
Keep track of the rhyme

Skip, skip, skip
Here and there
Skip, skip, skip
Not like a bear

Skip with one leg
Right or left leg
Take your time
and skip, skip, skip

PLANTING

Rake the ground.
Prepare the land.
Till the dirt.
Wipe off shirt

Wet the soil.
Watch the soup boil.
Work and toil.
Call friend Doyle.

Dig a trench.
Clear off any stench.
Sit on a bench,
You and a mensch.

Drop the seeds in.
Cover with good mix.
Stick a sign on a pin.
Check the soup to fix.

Let a few days pass.
The plants will grow fast.
Call Doyle and bask.
Eat tomatoes for breakfast.

Enjoy the harvest.
The fruits of your labor.
You planted the best.
Now you can savor.

BEDTIME

Snug in bed
Favorite book read
Tucked
Hugged
Patted
Kissed

Listen to house sounds –
soothing music
murmurs
T.V.'s on
water running
Eyes wide open
Sounds – loud and clear

Listen to street sounds –
cyclist passing
cars starting
runner sprinting
sirens wailing
Eyes slightly open
Muffled sounds

Listen to night sounds –
slight breeze
leaves rustling
cat growling
dogs barking
Eyes almost closed
Whispers

Listen to mind sounds –
running footsteps
chatting friends
whistling teapot
slamming doors
Eyes shut
Sounds come and go

Listen, listen with eyes shut tight
Listen for more sounds
Listen, listen...
Hear no sounds now...
no sounds left...

Quiet...
Still...

Good night!

MIMI'S PRAYER

Bless me.
Bless mommy and me.
Daddy too,
Nini and Manou.

I'll be good.
I'll eat all my food.
Thank you for Badood,
my cat, and dollie Lalood.

Thank you for today.
I don't know what else to say.
Thank you for Ray,
He came to play.

Mommy says it's nine.
She says my prayer's fine.
It's from my heart and from my mind;
And my prayer's all mine.

Good night now.
Badood, don't meow.
Get Manou, my cow.
Bring Nini, my sow.

Dum di doo di,
Bless me.
Mommy,
Daddy,
Me — Mimi.

NAME CHANGE

Mr. Stumble Bumble
tumbles
scrambles
fumbles
crumbles

He wasn't this way before;
He even had a different name.
His neighbors according to lore;
Reported before,
He was lame and tame.

Mr. Humble Mumble,
He was then.
Sat quietly with a pen.
Carried around a hen.
Slowly paced himself from one to ten.

And then one day, he had a fright!
His hen gave him a great big bite!
His pen couldn't open, it was closed tight!
He fell and got up with all his might!

Good-bye, Mr. Humble Mumble,
Good riddance to you.

Hello, Mr. Stumble Bumble,
How do you do!

RHYMES

Kitty says, "meow."
The bat goes "pow!"
Mama shouts, "now!"
"Moo," moans the cow.

Sarah screams, "No!"
Baby babbles "Mo."
Policeman directs you to go.
Calesas go to and fro

Miko is "it."
Dress is a tight fit.
Puppies try to sit.
Horses gallop and git.

Barnacles collect.
Chains don't connect.

Spiders detect –
a delectable insect.

I love to rhyme.
It's about time,
to make some sense sublime,
for my wit to climb.

To share,
To dare,
To prepare,
So beware –

More rhymes could come;
I'll think of some...
Oh dear – none...
The rhymes are gone.

GOING TO THE PARK

Let's go to the park;
Mom said on a lark.
We have to go before it gets dark.

Let's go to the store first;
We need to buy a present for Little Ned.
Let's give it to him before he goes to bed.

Then we have to pass by the library,
to return the late books, you see;
otherwise, I have to pay a large fee.

Let's pick up Aunt Miranda;
She likes our company, Tara-Bara;
We'll laugh together – lalatatarara!

I'll prepare some cold tea,
Take some crackers for you and me.
We might need something to snack on, you see.

Is your backpack in the car?
Watch out for the tar.
Do you have your sweatshirt on?
Did you choose a Raffi song?

Well hurry; we'll be late.
It's not like we have a date.
We still have to go to the park.
We have to go before it gets dark.

FALSE ALARM

OOOOOOaOOOOOOah
Clang, clang, clang,
  clang, clang
Whmmmmmmmmm -
There's a fire
There's a fire
Where's the fire
Where's the fire
All this commotion
All is in motion
All the noise
People lose their poise

Necks straining
Neighbors milling
Children running
  to the site
Mothers hanging on to
  them tight.

OOOOOOaOOOOOOah
Clang, clang, clang,
  clang, clang
Whmmmmmmmmm -
Here are the firemen

Here are the firemen
Make room for the firemen
Make room for the firemen
There's the smoke
There's the smoke

Be calm, be quiet, the
  captain spoke
The fire will be out right
  away - we hope

They lined up in columns
water hoses steady - ready
They surrounded the house
water hoses steady - ready
And the firemen charged
  on
water hoses steady - ready

There's the smoke
There's the smoke

but -

where's the fire?
the fire?
yes, the fire?
what fire?

Why it's only smoke
It's only smoke
what smoke?
It's smoke from a
  boiling pot
left boiling away in a
closed room at that!

They broke the columns
ever ready, weary firemen
They prepared to return
  to the station
ever ready, weary firemen
It was all part of their
  day's work
weary, ever ready firemen
to put out the smoke from
  a boiling pot
left boiling away in a
closed room at that.

MOE AND ME

Gotta go!
Gotta go!
Gotta go with Moe.
He's a bit slow;
But he's my bro;
And I love him so!

Moe and me,
Like milk and a cookie
We laugh with glee.
He's a bumblebee!
Full of energy –
That's Moe and me!

Moe jumps.
We bump.
We end up with lumps.
We don't care.
We just dare –
To see who can last,
Being fast like a blast!

We'll run and sun.
We'll have fun!
We'll joke and pun.
We'll eat a bun
We'll run till we're gone.
Then to home – we're done!

RAIN

I love the rain!
the smell of the wet earth
the tapping on the roof
the way it looks
as it pours, pours, pours.

I curl up and read my favorite book.
By the window I look, look, look.
Drink some milk, some juice, some tea.
I eat some snacks and snuggle with blankie.

I love the rain!
so soft and quiet
sometimes loud and strong
Bring on the lightning;
the thunder too
They don't scare me nor bother me.
So don't let them do it to you too!

When the wind dies down;
and the rain has stopped;
I'm off, I'm gone
I run, run, run –
on the puddles
on the wriggly worms
on the mud
It's so much fun.
I can hardly wait for the rain, again.
I'm undone!

PARDON?

How do you catch a Glimpet?
When all you can glimpse is a snippet.
She flits and darts all the way to Tibet.
She returns with a supply of dried mini giblets!

Where can you find a Ninigong?
I need one to put luck on a gong.
The gong will not sound for a song, a song.
I need a Ninigong for a gong!

Do you want a pet Bimbim?
He likes to snuggle and hangs on a limb.
He just snuggles and likes it dim.
He snuggles; that's his scheme;
and he's as sweet as a hymn.

When did you last catch a Nanoo?
It floats topsy-turvy and dipsy-doo.
It grabs; It scratches; It shakes you too!
It's definitely not a good candidate for the zoo!

We need a partner for Sundance.
He will eat only if he can dance.
His favorite dance is the prance.
He wants another horse for the starting stance.

Move aside another Diboobe needs space.
Can't you see what he's got on his face?
It's covered with thick lace.
His ears are growing maize.
Diboobe's face looks like a maze!

GROWING UP

Tiggy Piggy is about fun.
He's not hurrying growing up.
He just loves to roll in the mud till sunup.
Then loves to bask in the sun.

Beenee Roocheemeenee
Can't wait to grow up soon.
Then he'll play his game.
He'll change his name.
He'll wake up at noon.

Kana Dilidoodi
Won't grow up, you see.
She's all metal, nuts and bolts.
She's not like you and me.

Louise is a tease.
Growing up is a breeze.
She dances pirouettes - freeze!
That's her life; she's a Meese!

The twins are not happy.
Big sister shouts "grow up!"
How can this be?
We're dolls, you see!.

Mary sits on the mat.
Grown up means she can tap.
Tap dancing is a zap.
She dreams tap on the mat.

SEASONS

Can you hear angels sing?
Can you see fairy wings?
Listen to Tinkies go ding-ding.
Flowers bling. Birds fling.

Look at the forest covered with snow.
Hear the cold winds blow, blow.
Check the lighted houses all aglow!
Happy holidays! Ho! Ho! Ho!

Beaches packed with bathers tanning.
Children, half-naked, running, running.
Tank tops, shorts, swimsuits for bathing.
Hot dogs, lemonades, days steaming.

Red, orange, brown motley leaves –
Trees become bare of their sleeves.
Chilly nights, muddy skies, harvest moon –
Apple cider, nuts, popcorn. Fall soon!

Seasons come,
Seasons go,
What would we do,
If this wasn't so.

Enjoy each season,
Each one of them,
Watch them dress up the Earth,
Be overwhelmed!
Nature bestows,
Nature glows.

QUESTIONS

Tell me, Tildy
Tell me, true
Will you jump in the pool?
If I jump with you?

Ask him, Leary
Ask him, clearly
Does he want to eat merely –
To beat the doldrums dreary?

Call her, Lara
Tell her you're sorry
You left with Clara
Did she catch the lorry?

Bye, says Sly
Bye to pie?
All pies? Oh my!
I won't last – I'll die!

Say little bumble bee
What does the buzzing do for thee?
Can you fly without the buzz?
Can you navigate without the fuzz?

What happened Jorgen?
What's the squawking in the pen?
Didn't Yoga give you Zen?
Calm down,
Relax,
You silly hen.

WHAT TO DO

In a canoe –
Sunscreen slather
Hat on head
Shorts, tank top, matter
Hot day, Ted

In a car –
Books to read
Songs to heed
Snacks you'll need
Patience, indeed

In an airplane –
Think of sleep
Watch a movie
Gameboy – bleep, bleep
Maybe a book – twiddle dee dee

In a tricycle –
Look about
Feel the heat
Don't shout
Go with the beat

On an elephant –
Sit up high
Watch the thigh
Don't slide
He'll glide

On a carabao –
Hang on tight
He won't bite
Wave off a flying pest
He'll lumber his best

<u>OUTSIDE</u>

I'll swat the fly
Squish the plum
Trample on my mom's pie
Bite my thumb

I'll hit the wall
Break the swing
Throw the ball
Do my thing

I feel anxy
Nasty
Naughty
Nervy

It's hot
I am shot
Hurt a lot
Stewing in a pot

I am bored at home
Can't read a tome
Jumpy as a gnome
Take me to a dome

Let's go out
I won't shout
I won't pout
I won't be a lout

I want to be happy
Not be naughty and nasty
There's lots of fun
Let's go play in the sun

I want to play
To dance and sing
Just fun today
To laugh and have a fling

NOT SOLAR

Shh, shh, tiptoe
Natalie must not hear us
See us
Feel us
She must not know we're here; the poor dear!

Hide in the bushes.
Fly in turbo mode.
Camouflage yourselves on the toad.

Keep your chatter on low.
Minimize fluttering to slow.
Shut your glimmer and glow.

Let Natalie sleep.
Go to dreamland deep —
Not a peep, not a peep...

Keep her safe and secure —
Our mission to procure —
Lots of fireflies for more stature —
To get ready to mature —
Silently, secretly, for departure

She doesn't know who we are —
That we are from another star —
That we came from afar —
Ready to return to another system —
Not lunar
Not solar

JUST FOR ME

I love rainbows
I love bells
Colored hair bows
Fresh bread smells

Catchy ditties
Funky songs
Soft cuddly kitties
Warm woolen longs

Sugar coated donuts
Platform boots
Neon polka dots
Grandfather's suits

Merry berry rockets
Banana split frost
Jingles in my pockets
Lipstick gloss

Twirling panda bear
Chewy gooey cheese
Fancy colors on my hair
Scratches on my knees

A few simple things
No fuss no blings
Just for me
Yippee! Tee hee!

LOVE YOU ALL

I'm Margaux
I'm three
I'm also called –
Victoria Rose
Swish-a-ling
Sing
Nanoosh
Teebuo
Singit
Cherie
Poupee
Darling
Babba

I answer to all these names!
My family loves me!
They make me happy!
The names come from their hearts.
Their hearts are full of love for me.
Love you all!
Love you back!
Love you more!

CPSIA information can be obtained
at www.ICGtesting.com
Printed in the USA
BVHW021706240419
546358BV00002B/4/P

9 781643 982922